Has Anyone Seen
WINNIE
and
JEAN?

E. B. McHenry

BLOOMSBURY
CHILDREN'S
BOOKS

For Peter

Winnie and Jean
have not been seen
since Tuesday, before tea.

They dug between the fence,
in the place where the roses had been.

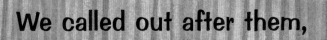

We called out after them,

"No, Winnie and Jean
are not at all mean.

And, yes! They wore vests
of plaid—blue and green."

Days passed while police

tracked where they HAD been . . .

. . . but Winnie and Jean

were not to be seen.

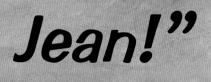

Winnie and Jean,
unleashed and unclean,
were free in a way
that they never had been.
They heard all the calls for them—

"Winnie!

Jean!"

Near the end of the week
they were chased off the green.

In her haste, Winnie tripped

and slipped
down a ravine.

Barking above her
for hours
was Jean.

This eventually brought
the police to the scene.

Officer Dean drove home
Winnie and Jean
and suggested we patch up
our fence with some screen

We did,
  and we're sure
    they can't dig in between . . .

Typeset in Impress BT
Art created with gouache
Book design by Amy Manzo Toth

Published by Bloomsbury U.S.A. Children's Books
175 Fifth Avenue, New York, NY 10010

Library of Congress Cataloging-in-Publication Data
McHenry, E. B.
Has anyone seen Winnie and Jean? / by E. B. McHenry. — 1st U.S. ed.
p.   cm.
Summary: Two corgi dogs escape from their owners and have
an exciting adventure before being returned home by the police.
ISBN-13: 978-1-58234-999-2 • ISBN-10: 1-58234-999-1
[1. Dogs—Fiction. 2. Stories in rhyme.] I. Title.
PZ8.3.M1597Has 2007   [E]—dc22   2006019898

First U.S. Edition 2007
Printed in China by South China Printing Company, Dongguan, Guangdong
3 5 7 9 10 8 6 4 2